MARC BROWN

D.W. SAYS PLEASE AND THANK YOU

Little, Brown and Company
New York Boston

For Isabella—talk about perfection!

Little, Brown and Company
Hachette Book Group
237 Park Avenue, New York, NY 10017
Visit our website at www.lb-kids.com

Little, Brown and Company is a division of Hachette Book Group, Inc.
The Little, Brown name and logo are trademarks of Hachette Book Group, Inc.

First Edition: April 2011
Originally published under the title *D.W.'s Guide to Perfect Manners*

D.W.® is a registered trademark of Marc Brown.

Library of Congress Cataloging-in-Publication Data

Brown, Marc Tolon.
[D.W.'s guide to perfect manners]
D.W. says please and thank you / by Marc Brown. — 1st ed.
p. cm.
Previously published in 2006 under title: D.W.'s guide to perfect manners.
Summary: D.W. shows how to be "perfect" for a day by demonstrating cleanliness, orderliness, and good manners.
Includes a self-test on manners.
ISBN 978-0-316-13077-6
[1. Behavior—Fiction. 2. Etiquette—Fiction. 3. Aardvark—Fiction.] I. Title. II. Title: DW says please and thank you.
PZ7.B81618Dwr 2011
[E]—dc22
2010038302

10 9 8 7 6 5 4 3 2 1
SC

Printed in China

My goofy brother, Arthur, dared me that I couldn't be perfect for one whole day. Well, I'll show him. Just watch me.

The first thing you need to do to be perfect is look perfect. Wash yourself, put on clean clothes, and comb your hair. Arthur said my teeth would turn green if I didn't brush them. I don't think that's true, but I brush them twice a day. Sometimes more.

I pick up my toys to make my room perfect. I can even make my own bed. You can, too. It's no big deal—and, besides, it freaks out your parents . . . in a good way!

Arthur says I'm always late for school or play dates. Well, even if I am late, I never forget to say "good-bye" when I leave.

I always say "hello" when I meet somebody. Nobody likes a grouch, so *smile* a little!

Perfect people say "I'm sorry" if they mess up or if they hurt someone. They don't say mean words like "shut up," "poopy," or "doo-doo head," even when bad things happen.

I almost forgot. If I sneeze or burp, I just say "Excuse me, please."
Even Arthur likes me then!

Don't forget to say "please" when you want something and "thank you" if you get it. Whining doesn't work—trust me, I've tried it. And don't grab things . . . like *some* people I know. The Tibble twins need serious help!

Being perfect means being careful with other kids' stuff. They won't want to play with you if you break things. Wait your turn, don't be a bully, and don't be bossy, either. Sometimes I have trouble with this one!

On the playground, follow the rules of the game so it doesn't get all crazy. Nobody likes a sore loser. If you're the winner, don't brag about it. And try not to laugh at people who make a mistake. You'll look like a baby!

Glass

Napkin

Spoon

Fork **Plate** **Knife**

Your parents will think you're great if you help out before meals by setting the table. Here's where everything goes.

And don't forget to wash your hands before you eat. If you have a brother like Arthur, you might have cooties!

Perfect people chew food with their mouths closed and never slurp their drinks.

I try everything on my plate . . . most of the time. It might *taste* good even if it doesn't *look* good—unless it's spinach!

If you spill something, help clean it up. And don't forget to say "sorry"!

When you're finished eating, ask if you may leave the table, instead of just walking away. If you're as old as I am, you can carry your dishes to the sink.

At night, it's not nice to complain about taking a bath or brushing your teeth. You can play while you get clean. Sometimes I play a little too hard!

At bedtime, instead of being a pain and saying "I'm not tired," I read books—even though I can't read yet! My parents *always* let me stay up to do that. Oh, and I almost forgot . . . Give the person who tucks you in a hug.

Good manners are so cool. They give you magical powers and people treat you like a big kid! And you know what? Being perfect isn't so hard. I might even try it again tomorrow.

Are You Perfect Yet? Try This Test and See!

1. Your neighbor offers you something to eat, but it looks really gross. What do you do?
   a. Say "yucky!" and stick out your tongue.
   b. Run away screaming.
   c. Say "thank you" and try a bite.

2. You want to play with your friend's brand-new toy. What do you do?
   a. Grab it and run away.
   b. Ask nicely and promise to be careful with it.
   c. Whine until your friend gives it to you.

3. You burp at the dinner table. What do you do?
   a. Say "excuse me."
   b. Say "Oops!" and hide under the table.
   c. Do it again.

4. Your parents tell you it's time for a bath. What do you do?
   a. Tell them you took one yesterday and you're still clean.
   b. Get your favorite bath toys and head to the tub.
   c. Hide under the bed.

5. You're done playing, and your toys are all over the floor. What do you do?
   a. Pick them up and put them away neatly.
   b. Wait for someone else to put them away for you.
   c. Get more toys out.

6. Your friend spills some milk. What do you do?
   a. Laugh and point to the puddle.
   b. Spill your milk too.
   c. Help clean up.

7. Someone says "good morning" to you. What do you do?
   a. Say "good morning" back.
   b. Grumble until you've had breakfast.
   c. Go back to bed.

8. It's time for bed, but you're not sleepy. What do you do?
   a. Say "good night," turn off the light, and try to go to sleep anyway.
   b. Ask for one more glass of water, one more story, or one more minute.
   c. Hide in the closet.

9. There's a long line for the slide at recess. What do you do?
   a. Cry.
   b. Wait your turn.
   c. Go home.

10. A new kid says "hello" to you. What do you do?
    a. Say "hello" and introduce yourself with a smile.
    b. Say "hello" and shake hands.
    c. Both a. and b.

Answers: 1. c   2. b   3. a   4. b   5. a   6. c   7. a   8. a   9. b   10. c

If you got **4 or fewer** answers right, you need a lot of work. Please read my book again.
If you got **5 to 7** answers right, you're getting there, but you need a little more practice.
If you got **8 to 10** answers right, wow! You're almost as perfect as I am!